"Everybody knows that, Daddy."

"Of course they do. But it's not well known that in those days bears and people sometimes fell in love and married each other. Their children were half human, half bear, so they became known as bear folk."

"I like hearing about them best," said Ursula.

"The bear folk were special," said Daddy, "because they could change their shape from one to the other whenever they wanted, which was very convenient for catching fish and climbing trees, and for sewing clothes and learning to draw."

"I want to marry a bear," said Ursula.

"That's not as easy as it used to be," said Daddy. "Nowadays nearly all bears have decided that they are better off staying away from people and living in the woods. And nearly all people have decided that they are better off staying away from bears and living in towns."

"Do you want to know a secret?"
Daddy whispered in his daughter's ear.
"Yes, please."
"Promise not to tell anyone?"
"I promise."

"Alright then. Now that people live in towns and bears live in the woods, have you ever wondered what happened to the bear folk?"

"Are there still bear folk, Daddy?"
"Oh yes," he said. "Once bears and people got mixed up they couldn't be unmixed up."
"And are there still bear children, Daddy?"
"Yes, but you have to look for them…"

"Some bear cubs like to slip away from the woods, change shape and visit towns. You see them in the park sometimes, playing with children."

"What about children? Do they change shape and play with bear cubs in the woods?"

"Some do," said Daddy. "Usually at night when their parents think they are tucked up in bed, dreaming."

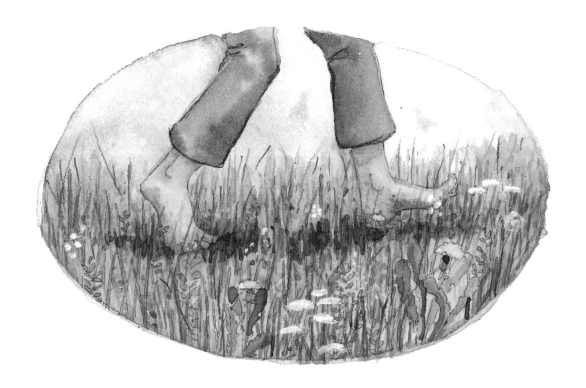

"I dream about playing with bears sometimes," said Ursula.
"Do you think I could be a bear child?"

"Mmmm, let's see… They love to walk barefoot through long grass."

"I hate wearing shoes," said Ursula.

"They are extremely clever
and ask lots of questions."

"I know all about numbers and stories
and animals and places," said Ursula.

"They are sturdy and strong,
not skinny-malinky-long-legs."
"I'm very strong," said Ursula,
hugging her daddy extra tight.
"So you are."

"Bear children love teddy bears and they have lots of them."

"I've got dozens," said Ursula. "I'm going to write a book about them one day."

"They love to eat," said Daddy, "and their favourite food is..."

"Apple pie."

"I was just about to say apple pie."

"With cream."

"Of course with cream," said Daddy. "On the whole, bear children are as nice as pie too, but they can be very fierce when they get angry."

"Grrrr," growled Ursula.

"What do bear children do when they grow up, Daddy?"

"That depends," he said. "Some never find out what they really are, but the ones who discover their inner bear do amazing things."

"What sorts of things?"

"All sorts. They travel far and wide. They read lots of books.
They collect interesting stuff. They run and swim and ski.
They grow things in their gardens and look after the world.
They have lots and lots of friends and they laugh a lot."

"More, Daddy. Tell me more."
"Let's see… Well, they make wonderful dens,
and they like to spend time with other creatures.
They are cooks and clowns and artists and teachers."

"Do they get married and have children?" said Ursula.

"Sometimes they do and sometimes they don't," said Daddy. "But they are all adventurous and they have extraordinary lives."

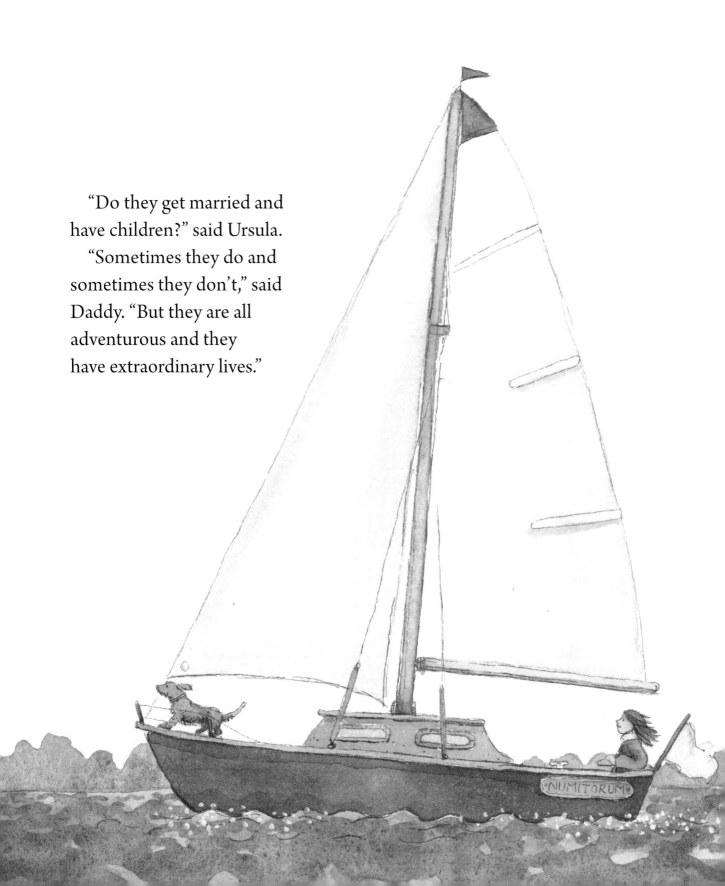

"Daddy...?"

"Yes..."

"Do bear folk live forever?"

"In our world no one lives forever, sweetheart.
We come here for a time and then we go back home."

"Where is home for bear folk, Daddy?" asked Ursula,
with a puzzled frown. "How do they get back there?"

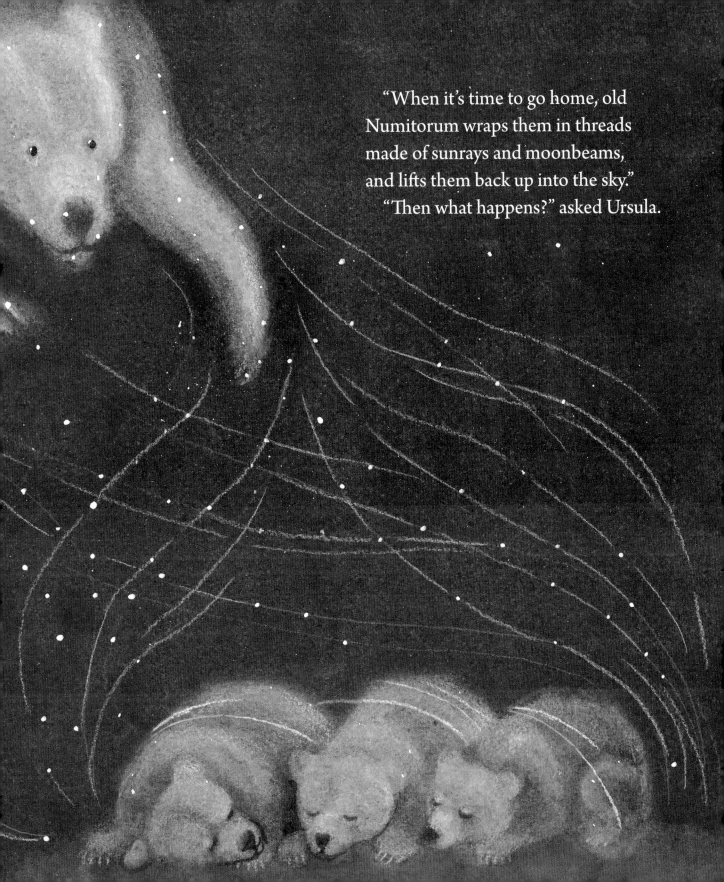

"When it's time to go home, old
Numitorum wraps them in threads
made of sunrays and moonbeams,
and lifts them back up into the sky."
"Then what happens?" asked Ursula.

"He gives them a big hug that lasts for a hundred years," replied Daddy, giving her a squeeze. "Then he sends them off to play among the stars with all the other bears who have come home."

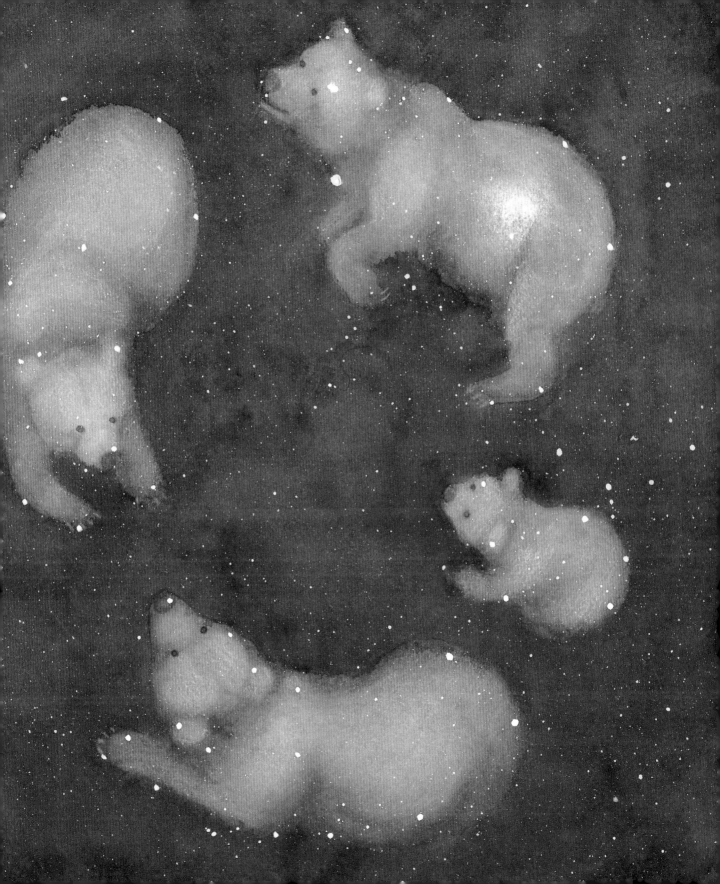

"I'd like that," said Ursula, yawning. Her eyelids drooped, her voice trailed off and she was fast asleep.

"So would I, sweetheart," said Daddy, scratching a tuft of fur behind his ear. "So would I."